To Mama and Papa, who gave me room to find my wings and the courage to fly. Your fearless pursuit of the wildest projects showed me how to dream big. Your love for books and the magic between their pages made me the author and artist I am today. Thank you for being the compass that's always pointing to true North.

I'll be forever grateful.

Published in association with
Bear With Us Productions

ISBN: 978-1-7370974-1-9

Cover by Richie Evans
Design by Luisa Moschetti
Illustrated by Caner Soylu

www.justbearwithus.com

ILLUSTRATED BY
CANER SOYLU

THE TROLL CASE FILES :

GRUFF

WRITTEN BY
ALICIA LOTT

Just beyond the forest edge, where busy
bees bounce on the breeze,
the sleepy road to Jubilee leads on with
songbirds in the trees.

There, on the banks of Bayou Creek,
still sits the tufted, twiggy throne
of a troll who **lost his bridge**
in the oldest tale this town has known.

He barely stands ten tacos tall;
his scruffy beard has grown for years.
And since his voice is big and booming,
when he laughs, he holds his ears.

He scales tall trees with ease
because he's fast and nimble as a fox.
He's really quite distinctive, from his
shaggy hair down to his socks!

"Hello there, friend,
my name is **Deklyn.**

Here's my story for today
about the time that I got famous
for one tiny no-good day."

"Ignore the books that say I'm bad.
You'll see they've got my story wrong.

So, just sit tight, and you will see
**I've been the good guy
all along!"**

"When Lantern fest was coming up,
I saw my bridge was breaking down.

So, I worked hard to get it ready
as the crowds poured into town.
I tightened ropes and straightened rails.

I sealed the planks - both front and back,
When, out of nowhere came the sound of:
CLIP-clop, CLIP-clop, CLIP- CRACK!"

"Oh I had heard that sound before.
It was those billy goats from Gruff who busted up my other
bridge. But, not **this** time- I'd had enough! You see, the problem
with those goats is that there's nothing they won't eat.

**In fact, they chew and chew until
they eat the dirt beneath their feet."**

"That day, I watched them hush and huddle,
with their hungry eyes gone wide.
They planned to come and eat **my meadow**
that I'd grown with care and pride!"

CLIP-clop

CLIP-clop

"I had to run and stop them soon
before they'd turn my grass to dirt
I crossed the bridge
and squared my shoulders
in my biggest, 'baddest' shirt.".

"The first one, **Baby Billy**,
came out whistling
happy as could be.

I stomped my feet and
boomed my loudest,

'Who's that, come
to bother me?'"

"Since you clip-*CLOPPED* across my bridge,
with hooves that crack and break the wood,
Just tell me why I shouldn't eat you -
and be done with you for good!'"

"Billy rubbed his chin and blinked,
then gave the answer he had come to:
You don't want to eat me, Troll.
My **brother**'s bigger. **He** will fill you!'"

"Now, I've never eaten goats,
but it was time for them to learn.
To cross my bridge would be a
prize that only friends of mine
could earn."

"Along came **Bigger
Brother Billy**, from his
post behind a tree.

I stomped my feet and boomed my loudest,

'Who's that, come to bother me?'"

"Since you clip-*CLOPPED* across my bridge,
with hooves that crack and break the wood,
Just tell me why I shouldn't eat you -
and be done with you for good!'"

"Billy rubbed his chin and blinked,
then gave the answer he had come to:
You don't want to eat me, Troll.
My **brother's** bigger. **He** will fill you!'"

"Still, I had to stop these kids,
so I dug deep to hatch a plan.
But then came Biggest Brother Billy...
more like Billy: Full-Grown Man."

"The bridge swung every time he stepped,
until we slid and hit the side.
I grabbed the ropes and held on tight
because I had no place to hide

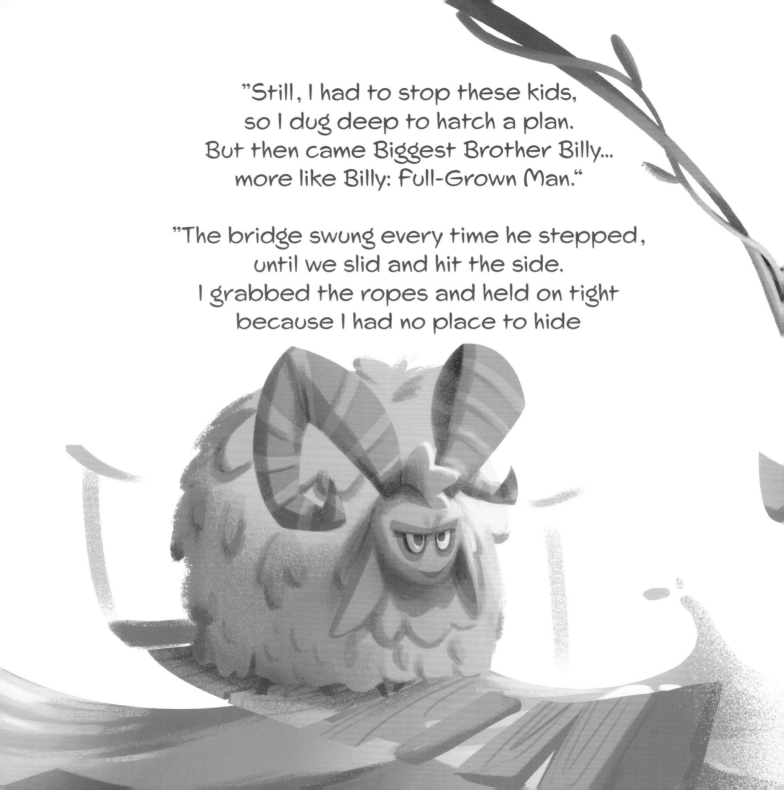

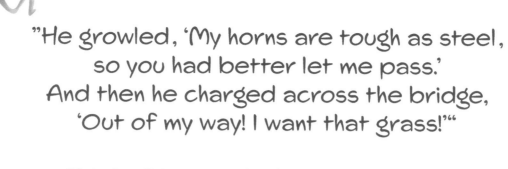

"He growled, 'My horns are tough as steel,
so you had better let me pass.'
And then he charged across the bridge,
'Out of my way! I want that grass!'"

"With all his weight, **he sent me flying,**
with a flip beyond the rail.
I floated off and sadly whispered,
'Even good plans sometimes fail.'"

"When I had floated long enough, I wrung my clothes and stepped ashore. I noticed lots of friendly faces - then went on to find some more."

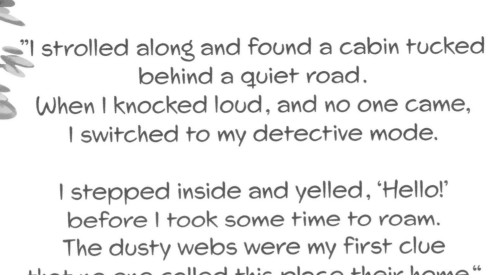

"I strolled along and found a cabin tucked
behind a quiet road.
When I knocked loud, and no one came,
I switched to my detective mode.

I stepped inside and yelled, 'Hello!'
before I took some time to roam.
The dusty webs were my first clue
that no one called this place their home."

"I found a creaky shed with
all the tools I'd need to cut the grass.
I raked the garden back to life
and scrubbed the doorknobs back to brass."

"So, by the time the sun went down,
I had a home that fit just right.
I roasted 'smores with my new neighbors
on the fire-pit that night."

"That 'bully-goat' had pushed me,
and he even thought he got his way.
And yet, our story wasn't done yet.
I knew just how to make him pay.

I called the sheriff with the facts
and said I might just sell my field -
if Biggest Brother paid my price
and told the town our case was sealed."

"Since my name has made me famous,
with my super-sleuthing ways
I take on cases for new clients who've had tiny,
no-good days. All their stories have old files
with missing facts that shed some doubt.

So, come along, I'll need your help
to find new clues and check them out."

"How many stories missed one side
before they made it to a book?
We'll have to work to dig them up
and give them all a second look."

"Now with your help, detectives,
I just know we'll solve each Troll Case File.
Let's meet our newest client now,
and pull the next one from the pile."